TWO TALES OF
SHEM AND SHAUN

TWO TALES OF SHEM AND SHAUN

FRAGMENTS FROM
WORK IN PROGRESS

BY

JAMES JOYCE

LONDON
FABER AND FABER
24 RUSSELL SQUARE

FIRST PUBLISHED IN DECEMBER MCMXXXII
BY FABER AND FABER LIMITED
24 RUSSELL SQUARE LONDON W.C.1
PRINTED IN GREAT BRITAIN BY
R. MACLEHOSE AND COMPANY LIMITED
THE UNIVERSITY PRESS GLASGOW

CONTENTS

7

THE MOOKSE
AND THE GRIPES

THE MOOKSE
AND THE GRIPES

*   *   *

Eins within a space and a weary wide
space it wast ere wohned a Mookse.
The onesomeness wast alltolonely,
archunsitslike, broady oval, and a Mookse
he would a walking go (My hood! cries An-
tony Romeo) so one grandsumer evening,
after a great morning and his good supper of
gammon and spittish, having flabelled his
eyes, pilleoled his nostrils, vacticanated his
ears and palliumed his throats, he put on
his impermeable, seized his impugnable,
harped on his crown and stepped out of his

immobile *De Rure Albo* (socolled becauld it was chalkfull of masterplasters and had borgeously letout gardens strown with cascadas, pintacostecas, horthoducts and currycombs) and set off from Ludstown *a spasso* to see how badness was badness in the weirdest of all pensible ways. As he set off with his father's sword, his *lancia spezzata*, he was girded on, and with that between his legs and his tarkeels, our once in only Bragspear, he clanked, to my clinking, from veetoes to threetop, every inch of an immortal. He had not walked over a pentiadpair of parsecs from his azylium when at the turning of the Shinshone Lanteran near Saint Bowery's-without-his-Walls he came (secunding to the one one oneth of the propecies, *Amnis Limina Permanent*) upon the most unconsciously boggylooking stream he ever locked his eyes with. Out of the colliens it took a rise by daubing itself Ninon. It looked little and it smelt of brown and it thought in narrows and it talked showshallow. And as it rinn it dribbled like any lively purliteasy: *My, my, my! Me and me! Little down dream don't I love thee!* And, I declare, what was there on the yonder bank of the stream that would be a river, parched on a limb of the olum, bolt downright, but the Gripes? And no doubt he was fit to be dried for why had he not been having the juice of his times?

His pips had been neatly all drowned on him; his polps were charging odours every older minute; he was quickly for getting the dresser's desdaign on the flyleaf of his frons; and he was quietly for giving the bailiff's distrain on to the bulkside of his *cul de Pompe*. In all his specious heavings, as be lived by Optimus Maximus, the Mookse had never seen his Dubville brooder-on-low so nigh to a pickle.

Adrian (that was the Mookse now's assumptinome) stuccstill phiz-à-phiz to the Gripes in an accessit of aurignacian. But Allmookse must to Moodend much as Allrouts, austereways or wastersways, in roaming run through Room. Hic sor a stone, singularly illud, and on hoc stone Seter satt huc sate which it filled quite poposterously and by acclammitation to its fullest justotoryum and whereopum with his unfallable encyclicling upom his alloilable, diupetriark of the wouest, and the athemystsprinkled pederect he always walked with, *Deusdedit*, cheek by jowel with his frisherman's

14

blague, *Bellua Triumphanes*, his everyway addedto wallat's collectium, for yea longer he lieved yea broader he betaught of it, the fetter, the summe and the haul it cost, he looked the first and last micahlike laicness of Quartus the Fifth and Quintus the Sixth and Sixtus the Seventh giving allnight sitting to Lio the Faultyfindth.

— Good appetite us, sir Mookse! How do you do it? cheeped the Gripes in a wherry whiggy maudelenian woice and the jackasses all within bawl laughed and brayed for his intentions for they knew their sly toad lowry now. I am rarumominum blessed to see you, my dear mouster. Will you not perhopes tell me everything if you are pleased, sanity? All about aulne and lithial and allsall allinall about awn and liseias? Ney?

Think of it! O miserendissimest retemp-
ter! A Gripes!

— Rats! bullowed the Mookse most tele-
sphorously, the concionator, and the sissy-
musses and the zozzymusses in their roben-
hauses quailed to hear his tardeynois at all
for you cannot wake a silken noise out of a
hoarse oar. Blast yourself and your ana-
thomy infairioriboos! No, hang you for an
animal rurale! I am superbly in my supre-
mest poncif! Abase you, baldyqueens! Ga-
ther behind me, satraps! Rot!

— I am till infinity obliged with you,
bowed the Gripes, his whine having gone
to his palpruy head. I am still always having a wish on all my extremities. By the
watch, what is the time, pace?

Figure it! The pining peever! To a Mookse!

— Ask my index, mund my achilles, swell my obolum, woshup my nase serene, answered the Mookse, rapidly by turning clement, urban, eugenious and celestian in the formose of good grogory humours. Quote awhore? That is quite about what I came on *my* missions with *my* intentions *laudibiliter* to settle with *you* barbarousse. Let thor be orlog. Let Pauline be Irene. Let you be Beeton. And let me be Los Angeles. Now measure your length. Now estimate my capacity. Well, sour? Is this space of our couple of hours too dimensional for you, temporiser? Will you give you up? *Como? Fuert it?*

Sancta Patientia. You should have heard the voice that answered him. *Culla vosellina.*

— I was just thinkling upon that, swees Mookse, but, for all the rime on my raisins, if I connow make my submission, I cannos give you up, the Gripes whimpered from nethermost of his wanhope. Ishallassoboundbewilsothoutoosezit. My tumble, loudy bullocker, is my own. My velicity is too fit in one stockend. And my spetial inexshellsis the belowing things ab ove. But I will never be abler to tell Your Honoriousness (here he near lost his limb) though my corked father was bott a pseudowaiter, whose o'cloak you ware.

Incredible! Well, hear the inevitable.

— *Your* temple, *sus in cribro!* Semperexcommunicambiambisumers. Tugurios-in-Newrobe or Tukurias-in-Ashies. Novarome, my creature, blievend bleives. My building space in lyonine city is always to let to leonlike Men, the Mookse in a most consistorous allocution pompifically with immediate jurisdiction constantinently concludded (what a crammer for the shape-wrucked Gripes!). And I regret to proclaim that it is out of my temporal to help you from being killed by inchies, (what a thrust!), as we first met each other newwhere so air-ly. (Poor little sowsieved subsquashed Gripes! I begin to feel contemption for him!). My side thank decretals, is as safe as motherour's houses, he continued, and I can seen from my holeydome what it is to be wholly sane. Unionjok and be joined to yok! Parysis, *tu sais*, crucycrooks, belongs to him who parises himself. And there I must leave you subject for the pressing. I can prove that against you, weight a mo-mentum, mein goot enemy! or Cospol's not our star. I bet you this dozen odd. This fo-luminous dozen odd. *Quas primas*—but 'tis

19

bitter to compote my knowledge's fructos of. Tomes.

Elevating, to give peint to his blick, his jewelled pederect to the allmysty cielung, he luckystruck blueild out of a few should-be santillants, a cloister of starabouts over Maples, a lucciolys in Teresa street and a stopsign before Sophy Barratt's, he gaddered togodder the odds docence of his vellumes, gresk, letton and russicruxian, onto the lapse of his prolegs, into umfullth onescuppered, and sat about his widerproof. He proved it well whoonearth dry and drysick times, and *vremiament, tu cesses*, to the extinction of Niklaus altogether (Niklaus Alopysius having been the once Gripes's popwilled nimbum) by Neuclidius and Inexagoras and Mumfsen and Thumpsem, by Orasmus and by Amenius, by Anacletus

the Jew and by Malachy the Augurer and
by the Cappon's collection and after that,
with Cheekee's gelatine and Alldaybran-
dy's formolon, he reproved it ehrltogether
when not in that order sundering in some
different order, alter three thirty and a
hundred times by the binomial dioram and
the penic walls and the ind, the Inklespill
legends and the rure, the rule of the hoop
and the blessons of expedience and the jus,
the jugicants of Pontius Pilax and all the
mummyscrips in Sick Bokes' Juncroom
and the Chapters for the Cunning of the
Chapters of the Conning Fox by Tail.

While that Mooksius with preprocession
and with proprecession, duplicitly and di-
plussedly, was promulgating ipsofacts and
sadcontras this raskolly Gripos he had all-
bust seceded in monophysicking his illso-

21

bordunates. But asawfulas he had caught his base semenoyous sarchnaktiers to combuccinate upon the silipses of his aspillouts and the acheporeoozers of his haggyown pneumax to synerethetise with the breadchestviousness of his sweeatovular ducose sofarfully the loggerthuds of his sakellaries were fond at variance with the synodals of his somepooliom and his babskissed nepogreasymost got the hoof from his philioquus.

— Efter thousand yaws, O Gripes con my sheepskins, yow will be belined to the world, enscayed the Mookse.

— Ofter thousand yores, amsered the Gripes, be the goat of MacHammud's, yours may be still, O Mookse, more botheared.

— Us shall be chosen as the first of the

last by the electress of Vale Hollow, obsel-
ved the Mookse nobily, for par the unicum
of Elelijiacks, Us am in Our stabulary and
that is what Ruby and Roby fall for, blis-
sim.

The Pills, the Nasal Wash (Yardly's),
the Army Man Cut, as british as bondstrict
and as straightcut as when that broken-
arched traveller from Nuzuland....

— Wee, cumfused the Gripes limply,
shall not even be the last of the first, wee
hope, when oust are visitated by the Veiled
Horror. And, he added: Mee are relying en-
tirely, see the fortethurd of Elissabed, on
the weightiness of mear's breath. Puffut!

Unsightbared embouscher, relentless foe
to social and business succes! (Hourihal-
eine) It might have been a happy evening
but....

And they viterberated each other, *canis et coluber* with the wildest ever wielded since Tarriestinus lashed Pissasphaltium.

— Unuchorn!

— Ungulant!

— Uvuloid!

— Uskybeak!

And bullfolly answered volleyball.

Nuvoletta in her lightdress, spunn of sisteen shimmers was looking down on them, leaning over the bannistars and listening all she childishly could. How she was brightened when Shouldrups in his glaubering hochskied his welkinstuck and how she was overclused when Kneesknobs on his zwivvel was makeacting such a paulse of himshelp! She was alone. All her nubied companions were asleeping with the squirrels. Their mivver, Mrs Moonan, was off in the Fuerst

24

quarter scrubbing the backsteps of Number 28. Fuvver, that Skand, he was up in Norwood's sokaparlour, eating oceans of Voking's Blemish. Nuvoletta listened as she reflected herself, though the heavenly one with his constellatria and his emanations stood between, and she tried all she tried to make the Mookse look up at her (but *he* was fore too adiaptotously farseeing) and to make the Gripes hear how coy she could be (though he was much too schystimatically auricular about *his ens* to heed her) but it was all mild's vapour moist. Not even her feignt reflection, Nuvoluccia, could they toke their gnoses off for their minds with intrepifide fate and bungless curiasity, were conclaved with Heliogobbleus and Commodus and Enobarbarus and whatever the coordinal dickens they

did as their damprauch of papyrs and bu-
chstubs said. As if that was their spiration!
As if theirs could duiparate her queendim!
As if she would be third perty to search on
search proceedings! She tried all the win-
some wonsome ways her four winds had
taught her. She tossed her sfumastelliaci-
nous hair like *la princesse de la Petite Bre-
tagne* and she rounded her mignons arms
like Mrs Cornwallis-West and she smiled
over herself like the beauty of the image of
the pose of the daughter of the queen of the
Emperour of Irelande and she sighed after
herself as were she born to bride with Tris-
tis Tristior Tristissimus. But, sweet mado-
nine, she might fair as well have carried her
daisy's worth to Florida. For the Mookse, a
dogmad Accanite, were not amoosed and
the Gripes, a dubliboused Catalick, wis

pinefully obliviscent. I see, she sighed.
There are menner.

The siss of the whisp of the sigh of the
softzing at the stir of the ver grose O arun-
do of a long one in midias reeds: and shades
began to glidder along the banks, greepsing, greepsing, duusk unto duusk, and it
was as glooming as gloaming could be in
the waste of all peacable worlds. Metamni-
sia was allsoonome coloroform brune; cithe-
rior spiane an eaulande, innemorous and un-
numerose. The Mookse had a sound eyes
right but he could not all hear. The Gripes
had light ears left yet he could but ill see.
He ceased. And he ceased, tung and trit,
and it was neversoever so dusk of both of
them. But still Moo thought on the deeps
of the undths he would profoundth come
the morrokse and still Gri feeled of the

scripes he would escipe if by grice he had luck enoupes.

O, how it was duusk! From Vallee Maraia to grasyaplaina, dormimust Echo! Ah dew! Ah dew! It was so duusk that the tears of night began to fall, first by ones and twos, then by threes and fours, at last by fives and sixes of sevens, for the tired ones were wecking, as we weep now with them. *O! O! O! Par la pluie!*

Then there came down to the thither bank a woman of no appearance (I believe she was a Black with chills at her feet) and she gathered up his hoariness the Mookse motamourfully where he was spread and caried him away to her invisible dwelling, thats hights, *Aquila Rapax*, for he was the holy sacred solem and poshup spit of her bushop's apron. So you see the Mookse he had reason as I knew and you knew and he knew all along. And there came down to the hither bank a woman to all important (though they say that she was comely, spite the cold in her heed) and, for he was as like it as blow it to a hawker's hank, she plucked down the Gripes, torn panicky autotone, in angeu from his limb and cariad away its beotitubes with her to her unseen shieling, it is, *De Rore Coeli*. And so the poor Gripes got wrong; for that is always how a Gripes is, always was and always will be. And it was never so thoughtful of either of them. And there were left now an only elmtree and but a stone. Polled with pietrous, Sierre but saule. O! Yes! And Nuvoletta, a lass.

Then Nuvoletta reflected for the last time in her little long life and she made up all her myriads of drifting minds in one. She cancelled all her engauzements. She climbed over the bannistars; she gave a childy cloudy cry: *Nuée! Nuée!* A lightdress fluttered. She was gone. And into the river that had been a stream (for a thousand of tears had gone eon her and come on her and she was stout and struck on dancing and her muddied name was Missisliffi) there fell a tear, a singult tear, the loveliest of all tears (I mean for those who are "keen" on the pretty-pretty commonface sort of thing you meet by hopeharrods) for it was a leap-tear. But the river tripped on her by and by, lapping as though her heart was brook: *Why, why, why! Weh, O weh! I'se so silly to be flowing but I no canna stay!*

THE ONDT
AND THE GRACEHOPER

THE ONDT AND
THE GRACEHOPER

*   *   *

The Gracehoper was always jigging a jog, hoppy, on akkant of his joyicity, (he had a partner pair of findlestilts to supplant him), or, if not, he was always making ungraceful overtures to Floh and Luse and Bienie and Vespatilla to play pupa-pupa and pulicy-pulicy and langtennas and pushpygyddyum and to commence insects with him, there mouthparts to his orefice and his gambills to there airy processes, even if only in chaste, ameng the everlastings, behold a waspering pot. He

would of curse melissciously, by his fore
feelhers, flexors, contractors, depressors
and extensors, lamely, harry me, marry
me, bury me, bind me, till she was puce for
shame and allso fourmish her in Spinner's
housery at the earthsbest schoppinhour so
summery as his cottage, which was cald
fourmillierly Tingsomingenting, groped up.
Or, if he was not done doing that, improb-
ably he was always striking up funny fun-
ereels with Besterfarther Zeuts, the Aged
One, with all his wigeared corollas, albed-
inous and oldbuoyant, inscythe his elytri-
cal wormcasket and Dehlia and Peonia,
his druping nymphs, bewheedling him,
compound eyes on hornitosehead, and Auld
Letty Plussiboots to scratch his cacumen
and cackle his tramsitus, diva deborah,
(seven bolls of sapo, a lick of lime, two

spurts of fussfor, threefurts of sulph, a shake o' shooker, doze grains of migniss and a mesfull of midcap pitchies. The whool of the whaal in the wheel of the whorl of the Boubou from Bourneum has thus come to taon!) and with tambarins and cantoridettes soturning around his eggshill rockcoach their dance McCaper in retrophœbia, beck from bulk, like fantastic disossed and jenny aprils to, the ra, the ra, the ra, the ra, langsome heels and langsome toesies, attended to by a mutter and doffer duffmatt baxingmotch and a myrmidins of pszozlers pszinging. *Satyr's Caudledayed Nice* and *Humbly, Dumbly Sod We Awhile* but *Ho, Time Timeagen, Wake!* For if sciencium (what's what) can mute uns nought, 'a thought, abought the Great Sommboddy within the Omniboss perhops an artsaccord (hoot's hoot) might sing ums tumtim abutt the Little Newbuddies that ring his panch. A high old tide for the barheated publics and the whole day as gratiis! Fudder and lighting for ally looty, any filly in a fog for O'Cronione lags acrumbling in his sands but his sunsunsuns still tumble on. Erething above ground, as his Book of Breathings bed him, so as everwhy, sham or shunner, zeemliangly to kick time.

Grouscious me and scarab my sahul! What a bagateller it is! Libelulous! Inzanzarity! Pou! Ptah! What a zeit for the goths! vented the Ondt, who, not being a sommerfool, was thothfolly making chilly spaces at hisphex affront of the icinglass of his windhame, which was cold antitopically Nixnixundnix. We shall not come to party at that lopp's, he decided possibly, for he is not on our social list. Nor to Ba's berial nether this oldeborre's yaar ablong as there's a khul on a khat. Nefersenless, when he had safely looked up his ovipository, he loftet hails and prayed: May he me no voida water! Seekit Hatup! May no he me tile pig shed on! Suckit Hotup! As broad as Beppy's realm shall flourish my reign shall flourish! As high as Heppy's hevn shall flurrish my haine shall hurrish! Shall grow, shall flourish! Shall hurrish! Hummum.

The Ondt was a weltall fellow, raumybult and abelboobied, bynear saw altitudinous wee a schelling in kopfers. He was sair sair sullemn and chairmanlooking when he was not making spaces in his psyche, but, laus! when he wore making spaces on his ikey, he ware mouche mothst secred and muravyingly wisechairmanlooking. Now whim the sillybilly of a Gracehoper had jingled through a jungle of love and debts and jangled through a jumble of life in doubts afterworse, wetting with the bimblebeaks, drikking with nautonects, bilking with durrydunglecks and horing after ladybirdies (*ichnehmon diagelegenaitoikon*) he fell joust as sieck as a sexton and tantoo pooveroo quant a churchprince, and wheer the midges to wend hemsylph or vosch to sirch for grub for his corapusse or to find a hospes, alick, he wist gnit! Bruko dry! fuko spint! Sultamont osa bare! And volomundo osi videvide! Nichtsnichtsundnichts! Not one pickopeck of muscowmoney to bag a tittlebits of beebread! Iomiol! Iomiol! Crick's corbicule, which a plight! O moy Bog, he contrited, I am heartily hungry!

He had eaten all the whilepaper, swallowed the lustres, devoured forty flights of styearcases, chewed up all the mensas and seccles, ronged the records, made mundballs of the ephemerids and voracioused most glutinously with the very timeplace in the ternitary—not too dusty a cicada of neutriment for a chittinous chip so mitey. But when Chrysalmas was on the bare branches off he went from Tingsomingenting. He took a round stroll and he took a stroll round and he took a round stroll-again till the grillies in his head and the leivnits in his hair made him thought he had the Tossmania. Had he twicylched the sees of the deed and trestraversed their revermer? Was he come to hevre with his engiles or gone to hull with the poop? The June snows was flocking in thuckflues on

the hegelstomes, millipeeds of it and myrio-
poods, and a lugly tournedos, the Borabo-
rayellers blohablasting tegolhuts up to tet-
ties and ruching sleets off the coppeehouses
with an irritant, penetrant, siphonopterous
spuk. Graussssssss! Opr! Graussssssss! Opr!

The Gracehoper who, though blind as
batflea, yet knew his good smetterling of
entymology promptly tossed himself in the
vico, phthin and phthir, on top of his buzzer
and the next time he makes the aquinatance
of the Ondt after this they have met them-
selves it shall be motylucky if he will beheld
not a world of differents. Behailed His
Gross the Ondt prostrandvorous upon his
dhrone, in his Papylonian babooshkees, with
unshrinkables farfalling from his unthink-
ables, swarming of himself in his sunny-
room, sated before his comfortumble phul-

lupsuppy of a plate o'monkynous and a confucion of minthe (for he was a conformed aceticist and aristotaller) as appi as a oneysucker or a baskerboy on the Libido with Floh biting his leg thigh and Luse lugging his luff leg and Bienie bussing him under his bonnet and Vespatilla blowing cosy fond tutties up the large of his smalls. Emmet and demmet and be jiltses crazed and be jadeses whipt! schneezed the Gracehoper, aguepe with ptchjelasys and at his wittol's indts, what have eyeforsight!

The Ondt, that true and perfect host, was making the greatest spass a body could with his queens laceswinging for he was spizzing all over him like thingsumanything in formicolation, boundlessly blissfilled in an allallahbath of houris. He was ameising himself hugely at crabround and marypose, chasing Floh out of charity and tickling Luse, I hope too, and tackling Bienie, faith, as well, and jucking Vespatilla jukely by the chimiche. Never did Dorsan from Dunshanagan dance it with more devilry! The veripatetic imago of the impossible Gracehoper on his odderkop in the myre, sans mantis ne shooshooe, feather weighed animule, actually and presumptuably sinctifying chronic's despair, was sufficiently and probably coocoo much for his chorous of gravitates. A darkener of the threshold? Haru! Orimis, capsizer of his antboat, sekketh rede from Evil-it-is, lord of loaves in Amongded. Be it! So be it! Thou-who-thou-art, the fleet-as-spindhrift, impfang thee of mine wideheight! Haru!

The thing pleased him andt, andt andt,

He larved ond he larved onn he merd such a
nauses

The Gracehoper feared he would mixplace his
fauces.

I forgive you, grondt Ondt, said the
Gracehoper, weeping,

For their sukes of the sakes you are safe in
whose keeping.

Teach Floh and Luse polkas, show Bienie
where's sweet

And be sure Vespatilla fines fat ones to heat.

As I once played the piper I must now pay
the count

So saida to Moyhammlet and marhaba to
your Mount!

Let who likes lump above so what flies be a
full'un;

I could not feel moregruggy if this was
prompollen.

I pick up your reproof, the horsegift of a
friend,

For the prize of your save is the price of my
spend.

*Can castwhores pulladeftkiss if oldpollocks
    forsake 'em*

Or Culex feel etchy if Pulex don't wake him?

A locus to loue, a term it t'embarass,

These twain are the twins that tick Homo
    Vulgaris.

Has Aqileone nort winged to go syf

*Since the Gwyfyn we were in his farrest
    drewbryf*

*And that Accident Man not beseeked where
    his story ends*

*Since longsephyring sighs sought heartseast
    for their orience?*

*We are Wastenot with Want, precondamned,
    two and true,*

*Till Nolans go volants and Bruneyes come
    blue.*

*Ere those gidflirts now gadding you quit your
    mocks for my gropes*

An extense must impull, an elapse must elopes,

*Of my tectucs takestock, tinktact, and ail's
    weal;*

As I view by your farlook hale yourself to
my heal,

Partiprise my thinwhins whiles my blink
points unbroken on

Your whole's whercabroads with Tout's
trightyright token on.

My in risible universe youdly haud find

Sulch oxtrabeeforeness meat soveal behind.

Your feats end enormous, your volumes
immense

(May the Graces I hoped for sing your
Ondtship song sense!),

Your genus its worldwide, your spacest
sublime!

But, Holy Saltmartin, why can't you beat
time?

In the name of the former and of the
latter and of their holocaust. Allmen.